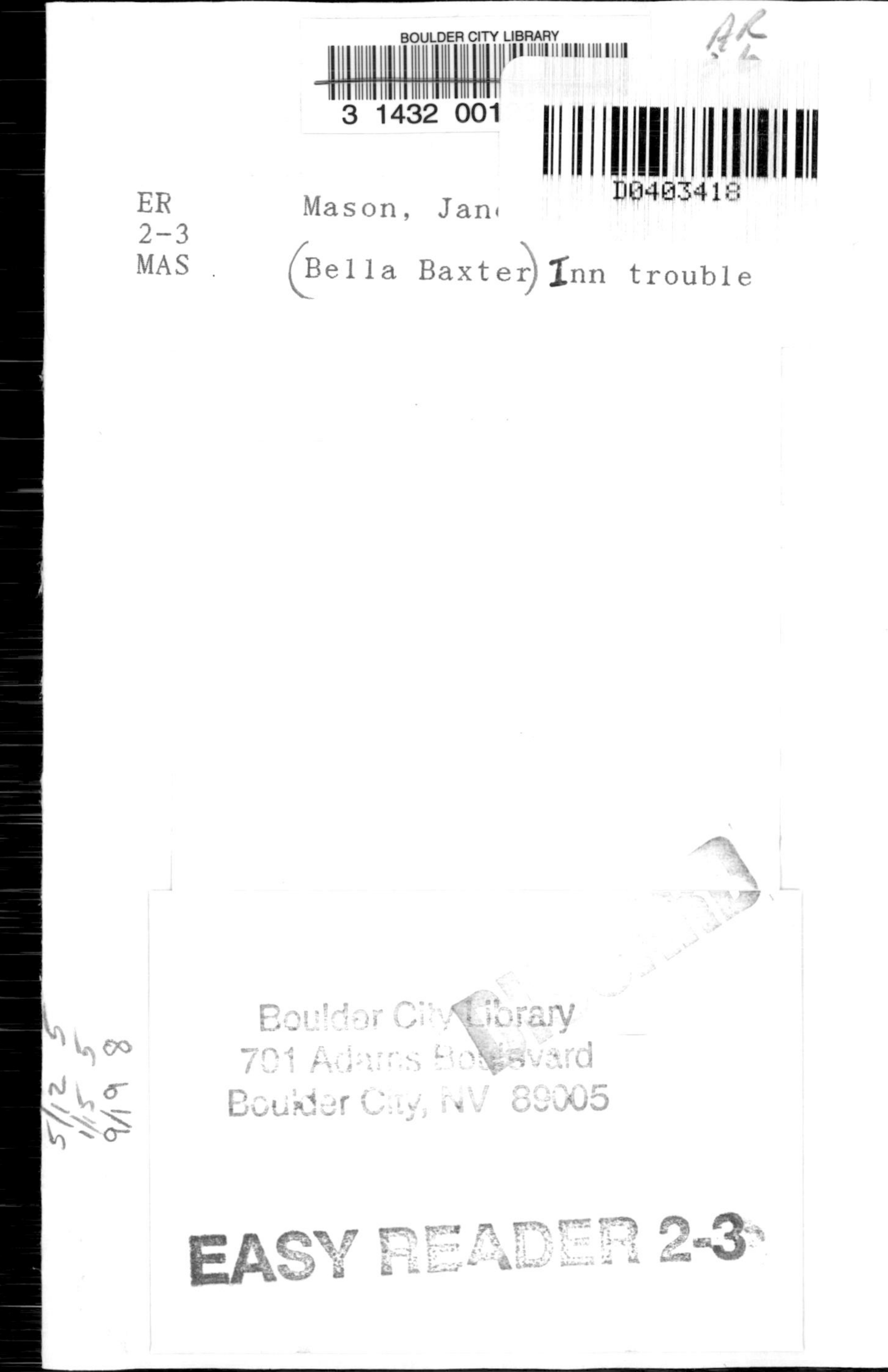

Bella Baxter # 1

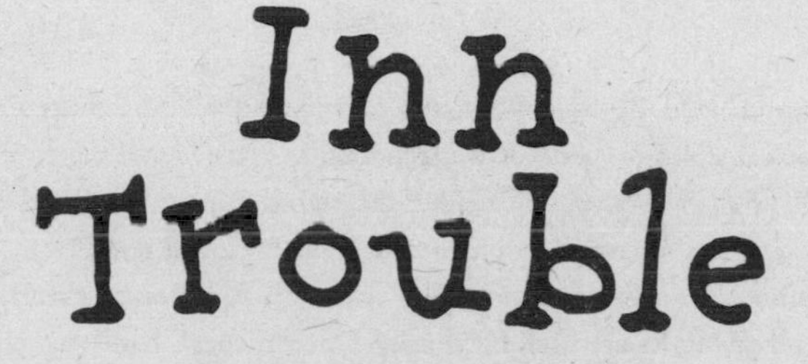

Inn Trouble

Jane B. Mason & Sarah Hines Stephens

Illustrated by John Shelley

Aladdin Paperbacks
New York London Toronto Sydney

For Brian —J. B. M.
For Nathan —S. H. S.

ALADDIN PAPERBACKS
An imprint of Simon & Schuster Children's Publishing Division
1230 Avenue of the Americas, New York, NY 10020

Designed by Debra Sfetsios
The text of this book was set in Baskerville Book.
Manufactured in the United States of America
First Aladdin Paperbacks edition June 2005
2 4 6 8 10 9 7 5 3 1
Library of Congress Control Number 2004109147

ISBN 0-689-86280-6 (pbk.)

Bella Baxter # 1

Inn Trouble

CHAPTER 1

Moving Inn

"Bella," a voice called. "Breakfast."

Isabella Baxter opened her eyes and let out a big puff of air. She was still getting used to waking up in her new room. And right now it was kind of . . . smelly. It smelled like a skunk.

Bella hopped out of bed. She shivered into her old school sweatshirt and one-hole jeans. Then she creaked down the l-o-n-g upstairs hall.

Bella's new house was Sea Inn–a bed and breakfast. It was like a hotel, only the guests shared the bathroom and a family lived there. Bella's family.

Wham! Bam! Bella could hear clunks and thunks coming from the kitchen. Since they'd moved in three weeks ago there'd been a lot of that. The B & B wasn't exactly in great shape. In fact it was kind of a disaster.

Bella peeked into the guest rooms as she passed. They were filled mostly with boards and buckets and paintbrushes.

One at the top of the stairs had crooked wallpaper hanging off the walls. Bella passed that room without looking in. She didn't want to see it. She just wanted it to go away.

Bella hurried down the stairs. She pushed open the swinging door to the kitchen. Her mother, Nellie, was standing at the stove. In one hand she held a spatula. In the other hand she held a hammer. A bandana covered her nose.

Wham! Nellie hit the hood over the stove with the hammer. "Darn you, fan! Work!" she shouted. "I could use some help around here, you know!"

Bella felt a twinge of guilt.

"Oh, good morning, sweetie," Bella's mom

said when she saw her daughter. She flipped a pancake. "Did you sleep well?" She raised the hammer again. Bella covered her ears. *Wham!*

The good news was her mom didn't seem mad about yesterday's wallpaper fiasco. But the stink in the kitchen was *awful.* How could anyone breathe in here?

At the table Bella's dad checked e-mail. Or tried to.

"Nellie, is there something wrong with the phone line?" he asked. He pushed his glasses back up his nose. "I can't get a connection. Oh, hi, Bella," he added, smiling her way.

Bella breathed through her mouth like she did when she and her dad went to the dump. Then she twirled to the kitchen table and kissed her dad on the cheek.

"Hi, Daddy." She picked up the phone cord and plugged it into the back of the computer. "Try it now."

Barnaby hit a button on the keypad and a dial tone echoed in the kitchen.

"Thanks, angel pie," Bella's dad said.

"Sure." Bella's dad was an amazing gardener. But he was terrible with anything mechanical. Or electronic. Since they'd moved to Sea Inn it seemed he'd broken more things than he'd fixed.

"The pancakes smell great, Mom," Bella said. "But that other smell . . ."

"The skunk. He moved in last night." Nellie's words were a little muffled because she had to talk through her bandana. She gave the stove hood another whack. This time the fan sputtered on, loudly.

"He must not like having us for roommates." Nellie shouted over the noise of the fan. She handed Bella a plate of steaming pancakes. "Here you go, Bella. If I were you, I'd eat on the porch."

Bella poured maple syrup onto her pancakes. Then she grabbed her juice and headed out to Sea Inn's wraparound porch.

Once outside Bella took a deep breath. The air outside was still a little skunky, but not too bad.

She set her plate on a little table and plopped down on the wicker chair beside it.

The porch was her absolute favorite part about Sea Inn. And Sea Inn had *lots* of parts. The creaky old house was huge. It had three parlors, which were kind of like living rooms. It also had two kitchens and a huge dining room. Plus eight guestrooms. And that didn't count Bella's or her parents' rooms.

Bella's mom said the house had tons of potential. Bella said it had tons of problems. The roof leaked. The bathroom tiles were loose. The electricity didn't work in some of the rooms. And most of the plaster was cracked.

And now there was a new problem–a skunk who thought the basement was an animal hotel!

CHAPTER 1

A Bad Breakfast

Bella picked up her fork. The pancakes looked delicious, and she was starved. She cut into the stack and stuffed a forkful into her mouth.

Ugh! They tasted like baking powder. Taking a big swig of juice, Bella washed the bite down. Then she sighed.

Her mom used to be the best cook ever. But since they'd moved to Sea Inn she hadn't cooked a single delicious meal. She was too worried about everything that needed to get done. Her dream had always been to own a bed and breakfast by the ocean. A place where everyone would want to stay.

They had the place by the ocean, all right. But who would want to stay in an inn with water leaks and crooked wallpaper?

Bella closed her eyes. She pictured the rose-covered wallpaper she'd hung the day before. In her mind's eye it was perfectly straight. But even though she hadn't looked in the room this morning, she knew better. That wallpaper was as crooked as the Tower of Pisa.

Bella had been trying to help. Her parents had way too much to do. Winning Sea Inn in an online contest had seemed like a dream. But getting it up and running was more like a nightmare. So Bella decided to help out and surprise her parents.

A magazine article about wallpapering was spread out on the floor next to the rolls of paper. It didn't look hard.

But hanging wallpaper was trickier than it seemed. Bella managed to get five pieces up. Most of them were kind of bumpy. And crooked. There were blobs of paste on the flowers.

When Nellie Baxter walked into the room her hands flew to her mouth. Even two hands weren't enough to cover up the loud moan that came out.

"We'll never get this place ready for guests," Bella's mom said sadly.

Barnaby put his hand on Bella's shoulder. Bella could tell she was about to get a lecture.

"We appreciate your help, Bella," her dad said in his serious voice. "But from now on maybe you should just try and enjoy your summer vacation."

Bella knew right then that she had messed up.

Bella stared down at her plate of salty pancakes. She knew her mom had plans for Sea Inn. She wanted to fill the rooms with fresh flowers and serve golden omelettes at her four-course breakfasts. But right now those plans seemed farther away than Bella's friends. And they were halfway across the state of Connecticut!

Sea Inn was a mess. And ready or not, the first guests were going to arrive in a week!

CHAPTER 3

Parents Gone Berserk!

Bella Baxter could do lots of things. Hanging wallpaper was not one of them. Neither was finishing her breakfast.

With a sigh Bella attempted another bite of baking powder pancake. Sometimes a big sigh helped Bella get over a grumpy mood. She sighed again, louder. But the big whooshing breaths weren't helping. She was missing too much.

She missed her house. She missed her street. She missed her friends.

Most of all Bella missed her normal parents. They were both going bonkers! Her mom was constantly talking to herself, and *the house*!

And her Dad! He was even worse. Bella counted on her fingers how many tumbles Barnaby had taken off ladders in the last week. She ticked off every finger on one hand and the thumb of her second.

Was six falls enough to cause permanent brain damage? Her dad definitely didn't seem normal.

Bella bit down on something hard–and splintery. Ugh! She spit a gritty bite over the porch rail into the daisies. Bella looked over her shoulder to make sure nobody was looking. Then she slid the rest of her breakfast into the flowers too.

Ptooey! Her mouth tasted like . . . wood! Was she actually eating a piece of roof shingle? Bella gazed up at the porch roof. She saw clear blue sky through a hole. Yup. She was!

Bella looked to make sure her pancakes weren't showing. They weren't. Then she headed inside.

"Great pancakes, Mom." Bella smiled. She dumped her dishes into the sink. Her mom muttered something to the wall socket.

"Hey, Dad, do you have your to-do list handy?" Barnaby looked up. He paged through several sheets on a yellow legal pad. Every line was filled.

"Yes," he said. It sounded like a yawn. "Find something else?"

"There's a hole in the porch roof," Bella reported. Barnaby nodded. He jotted something on his list. "Thank you, gumdrop," he said.

Even though her father said thank you, Bella felt terrible. The last thing he needed was another item on his list. She looked at the floor. It needed refinishing. Then she noticed something else. Barnaby's socks didn't match. He had on one plaid dress sock and one yellow striped tube sock. That proved it. He had gone around the bend.

Bella had no choice. She had to help whether her parents wanted her to or not.

She tapped her chin. What did an almost eight-year-old (even a really, really smart one) know about do-it-yourselfing? Her track record wasn't exactly stellar.

Still thinking, Bella backed out of the kitchen. Suddenly she slapped her forehead. She could *learn* about fixing houses! After all she was one of the fastest learners ever. And she knew exactly where to get the information she needed.

Bella raced upstairs. She sat down at her desk and pulled out a new stack of yellow Post-its. She pictured her dad's l-o-n-g list in her head. Then she made her own list.

When she was done she grabbed her back-pack and baseball cap.

"I'm going for a walk," she told her dad.

"Okay, tulip," he replied.

Bella bounded out the door. She was on her way!

CHAPTER 4

No Place Like Home

As Bella hurried down the sidewalk her money jingled in her pocket. Her backpack bounced on her back. Something rustled softly in her sweatshirt sleeve. And her feet felt light. She was ready to put her plan into action! Except for one thing–her stomach felt empty.

Lucky for Bella, Bruno's Bakery was on the way. She had gone there with her dad and remembered exactly where it was. And anyway, she could have followed her nose. The smells coming from the yellow-shingled building were all buttery and sugary.

Two cow bells clanged as Bella pushed open

the door. Inside were three small tables with chessboards painted on their tops and six comfy chairs. A dusty-looking baker stood behind a case of cookies, pies, and pastries.

"How can I help you, madam?" the man asked. His name was Bruno Benson. He was the owner.

Bella closed the door behind her and smiled. She wondered if Bruno's hair was really as powdery white as it looked or if it was just flour.

"Well, hello neighbor!" Bruno said when he recognized Bella. "How is the B & B coming along?"

Bella gave Bruno a serious look. She shook her head and sucked in her lips. "I think all of that potential is making my parents a little nuts," she confided.

"They have their work cut out for them, don't they?" The baker leaned on the counter and clucked his tongue.

Bella wasn't sure what he meant. But she nodded anyway. "Pretty soon I'll have their work all looked up for them too," she added.

Just then Bella's stomach growled. It sounded like an angry cat. Bella had to feed it, and fast.

She looked at all of the good things behind the glass. There were cinnamon buns and croissants and bear claws. There were sugar cookies and chocolate tarts and apple dumplings. Bella was too hungry to decide.

At last she pointed to a cinnamon bun. The baker slipped the sticky spiral of dough inside a white paper sack.

"Good choice," he said.

Bella slid her quarters across the counter. Bruno slid one back.

"Neighborhood discount," he said with a smile. Bella wanted to thank him, but her mouth was already full of cinnamon bun. Instead she smiled as best she could and waved good-bye.

Bella's mouth was happy. Her stomach was already quieting down. By the time she reached the double red doors she had licked the last crumbs of cinnamon sugar off her fingers. She was ready to get to work.

Bella marched up the stairs and pushed her way into the building that held all the answers.

The second Bella's feet hit the marble floor of the town library she felt different. Better. Sort of . . . relieved.

Bella breathed in the musty smell of old paper. She looked at the shelves and shelves of books. They looked familiar. Like friends. And suddenly Bella knew what the feeling was inside her. She felt at home for the first time since they'd moved to Sandyport.

Soothed by the rustling of turning pages, Bella walked toward a wall of books. She ran her hands along their spines. There were so many!

Maybe my parents and I can just move in here, Bella thought.

Bella carefully removed her sweatshirt. Small yellow Post-it notes were stuck to her arm. Her list. It wasn't as long as her dad's. But it reached from her shoulder to her wrist.

Bella pulled a couple of stray notes out of her sleeve. She stuck them close to her elbow. Then she spotted the information desk. That was always a good place to start.

"Hi," Bella said to the librarian behind the desk. "I'm looking for books on roof repair, electrical wiring, plaster repair, tile and grout, and how to get a skunk out of your basement," she read from her arm.

The librarian looked up from her card file. She had spiky hair and glasses. She peered over the top of her cat-eye frames and one of her eyebrows went up.

"Whoa, there, Annie Oakley," she said. "Let's rein this in and take it again. One question at a time. Exactly what kind of roof are we talking about? Shake? Tar? Tile? Tin?"

The librarian wasn't smiling. She looked friendly, but a little . . . sharp. Like a brand-new pair of scissors.

Bella was speechless. For exactly two whole seconds she couldn't think of anything to say. She had no idea there were so many kinds of roofs! She *had* to find out more about them. *All* of them!

CHAPTER 5

Books, Books, Books

"I'm not sure," Bella finally said. The words felt kind of funny. She hardly ever said them! She was about to tell the librarian, whose nametag said TRUDY, that she wanted books on all kinds of roofs. But just then Trudy thumped a finger against her forehead.

"Interesting," she said. She pulled open the card catalog. "Maybe we can find a book that covers several types. And some other fix-it projects, too. Let's take a quick look at the six hundreds."

Bella watched as the librarian flipped through the catalog. A computer hummed quietly on the

desk, but the librarian ignored it. "Six twenty, six ninety, six ninety-five, six ninety-eight . . ."

Her heart raced. Bella had a feeling Trudy was going to be a big help. She *definitely* knew how to do a catalog search. So far her plan was going great.

"Where would we be without Melvil Dewey?" Trudy said. She jotted a few notes down on a piece of scrap paper.

Bella grinned. Melvil Dewey invented the Dewey decimal system. He was practically her hero.

"Digging through piles and piles of unorganized books," Bella replied with a giggle.

Trudy giggled back. "Exactly." She put her finger on her nose to show Bella she was spot on. "Thanks to him, I've tracked down a few titles that might have what we need. And I know just where they are."

Trudy led Bella over to the 600s and began to pull books off the shelf. There was *Roofing for Rookies, Plaster Made Perfect, How to Tile without Having a Tizzy,* and more.

"These are perfect," Bella declared.

She and Trudy loaded up with the heavy volumes and trudged over to a large round table.

Minutes later they were busily flipping through the books. Bella started with *Roofing for Rookies,* and Trudy opened up *Infatuation with Restoration.*

Trudy pulled a collection of tiny clear, neon-tipped Post-its out of her pocket. Bella's eyes widened. She'd never seen Post-its like those!

"Help yourself," Trudy said. She pushed the pink ones across the table. Bella set them next to her and started to read about roofs.

"I think we have cedar shingles," Bella said after a few minutes. She'd found a picture of a roof that looked like Sea Inn's. "It looks pretty, but doesn't taste very good. I got a bite of it this morning."

"A bite?" Trudy raised one eyebrow for a second time.

Bella nodded. "I was eating out on the porch, and a piece of shingle fell right into my pancakes."

Trudy's eyebrows shot up over her glasses again. Both of them.

"It's okay," Bella assured her. "They were terrible anyway. Mom's a great cook, but not since we moved here. She's too worried about fixing up Sea Inn."

It felt good to be telling someone about what was going on. And Trudy really seemed interested. She was leaning across the table, her eyes wide.

"The pancakes were so bad I had to throw

them into the bushes!" Bella admitted. "Luckily Mom and Dad were in the kitchen, so they didn't see me."

Trudy nodded. Her hair spikes bobbed.

"After I chewed the roof I knew I had to do something," Bella went on. "Guests are coming in a week!"

"A week isn't much time," Trudy agreed. "Especially when it comes to a house as big as Sea Inn."

"You know Sea Inn?" Bella asked.

Trudy smiled. "Sure do," she said. "Everyone around here does."

Bella closed the roofing book and picked up *Plaster Made Perfect.* She flagged a few more pages, then moved on to *How to Tile without Having a Tizzy.*

Across the table, Trudy's nose was buried in electrical wiring. She looked like a fast learner.

Hours later Bella and Trudy had thoroughly covered all the subjects on Bella's arm. Except for skunk removal.

"You might have to call Joe Saunders about that," Trudy said as she checked out the last book in Bella's pile. "He's down at animal control. Just tell him I told you he's the man for the job."

"Okay," Bella said. She loaded up her backpack with books. They didn't all fit, and she had to carry several in her arms. Good thing Sea Inn was only a couple of blocks away.

"Thanks, Trudy," Bella said.

"You're welcome," Trudy said with a smile. "Come back and see me. Soon."

Bella grinned over the top of the stack of books. "I will. I promise." Bella waddled out the door. Even though her arms felt heavy with the weight of the books, she felt lighter than she had in days. She had more than enough information now. And she had something even better–a new friend!

Chapter 6

A Fresh Start

Bella panted as she staggered up the walk. She was walking slowly. The books in her arms were getting h-e-a-v-y.

Peering over the stack, she saw her dad on the roof. He was frowning. Bella could see flecks of paint in his hair.

"Hi, Daddy," she called up.

Barnaby Baxter looked down at his daughter and grinned. "Whatcha got there, sweet pea? Did you rob a bookstore?" He started to climb down the ladder.

"Careful, Daddy," Bella warned. She didn't want him to take another fall.

A minute later Barnaby stepped safely off the lowest rung. He strolled over to Bella and took a few of the books off her pile. "Looks like you could use a hand," he said. He gazed at the books in his daughter's arms and his eyes widened.

"Actually I thought *you* could use a hand. These are books on how to fix up Sea Inn," Bella said excitedly. She handed him the top book from the pile: *How to Fix Your House Up Without Having a Breakdown*. "I thought this one might be *really* good."

"Bella!" Barnaby said. He let out a little whoop. "These are great!" He reached for the rest of the stack and hurried into the house.

"I have more in my backpack!" Bella called after him. She shook out her tired arms and followed her dad inside.

By the time she got to the kitchen her dad was already spreading the books out on the kitchen table. Bella's mom was there too. She was wearing overalls and a T-shirt covered with blobs of plaster.

Bella took a quick whiff. The kitchen still

smelled skunky. But it was not as bad as it had been that morning.

"Look at this, Nellie!" Bella's dad crowed. "Bella paid a visit to the local library to get us some books. She even flagged the important pages!

"This calls for a new notebook!" He pulled a yellow pad out of a drawer and sat down. A second later his nose was buried in a chapter on roof repair.

"I think we have cedar shingles," Bella said.

"Um-hmmm," her dad replied.

Bella giggled. Her dad looked up.

"Thanks for getting these, gumdrop," he said. "They're going to be a big help."

"A very smart idea, Bella," her mom agreed. She pulled tomatoes and lasagna noodles out of the cupboard.

"Lasagna!" Bella said excitedly. She'd been so busy at the library she forgot to have lunch!

Her mom made *great* lasagna. Or at least she usually did. Bella decided to stick around and make sure she didn't overcook the noodles or put too much salt in the tomato sauce.

"I think I'll have a snack," Bella said. Over at the table her dad was mumbling about two-way and three-way light switches.

Bella was crunching away on a dry lasagna noodle when she remembered something.

"Where's the phone book?" she asked.

"In the drawer by the phone," her mom answered. "Why?"

"Oh, nothing," Bella replied. She thumbed through the phone book. Then she picked up the phone. It was an old one. It hung on the wall and had a really long stretchy cord that could reach across the kitchen.

Bella swung the phone cord like a jump rope.

The phone rang on the other end. Once. Twice. Three times.

Finally somebody picked it up. "Animal control," the voice said. "This is Joe."

"Hi Joe, I'm Bella," Bella said. "My parents and I just moved into Sea Inn and we have a skunk in our basement."

"A skunk, you say?" Joe replied. "Sounds like trouble. I can come over tomorrow morning. How about nine o'clock?"

Bella swung the cord really high. "That sounds good," she said. "See you then."

Bella hung up the phone. "That was Joe Saunders down at animal control. He's coming over tomorrow to get rid of the skunk."

"Nice work, Bella," her mom said as she stirred.

Bella pulled a chair up to the stove. She had forgotten to keep a close eye on her mom while she made the sauce. But it looked okay. It smelled okay too. The aroma of onions and garlic was even covering up the smell of skunk.

But Bella couldn't be sure it was good until she tasted it.

When the family sat down to dinner everything looked delicious. Bella smiled. Her mouth watered as she forked up her first bite. Closing her eyes, she stuffed it into her mouth. Then she chewed.

Hmm. What started out weird turned worse. The lasagna tasted kind of . . . well, refreshing.

"Oh no," Nellie moaned. "I think I used mint instead of oregano."

"And cardboard instead of noodle." Bella's dad struggled to swallow his first bite. The noodles were still hard.

Luckily the garlic bread and the salad were good. Bella quickly helped herself to more of those. Then she changed the subject.

"You have to see the library," Bella said, beaming. "It's so great! And the librarian I met there is even greater. Her name is Trudy. She knows everything about everything! Like did you know that those frosty-looking domed rooftops in

Russia are called onions? She told me that." Bella was talking fast.

"Trudy wears pointy glasses. She got them in New York," Bella went on. "She wears them on a zebra striped ribbon around her neck. And she looks at you over the tops of them like this."

Bella did her best imitation of Trudy.

"That's nice, sweetie," is all her mom said.

"You'll have to meet her someday," Bella finally said.

Barnaby Baxter nodded. "I'm sure that someday we will," he said.

CHAPTER 7

Someday

The next morning Bella woke up to the sound of a truck backfiring. For a minute she was confused. Was she back in Hartford with all of the traffic?

Ka-boom! There it was again, closer.

Bella threw back her covers and jumped out of bed. She peered out her window and blinked in surprise. It was Trudy! And she was driving a really old, really noisy pickup truck.

Bella threw on her clothes and sneakers. She was downstairs in two minutes—a new record.

When she got to the door Trudy was about to ring the bell. Only it didn't work, of course.

Bella opened the door as her parents came into the front hall. "Hi, Trudy!" she said. "Nice outfit."

Trudy was wearing overalls and a carpenter's tool belt. The belt was stocked with a hammer, nails, two screwdrivers, a tape measure, a wrench, and a small crowbar. She also had a highlighter, a notepad, chocolate chips, Post-its, and huge purple sunglasses.

"Hiya, toots," Trudy said. She stepped into the foyer. Looking around, she inhaled sharply, then sniffed.

"Are you allergic to dust?" Bella asked. She knew people with allergies got watery noses.

"Oh, no," Trudy said. She wiped her eyes and stepped forward. "You must be Bella's parents. I'm Trudy Steiner." She shook Bella's dad's hand so hard Bella thought it might fall off.

"I'm so glad such a terrific family has moved into my great-grandfather's house."

Bella's mouth dropped open. Her parents looked surprised too. Sea Inn used to belong to Trudy's great-grandfather!

Trudy was still talking. "Since it's my day off, I thought I'd come over and lend a hand."

Bella's dad was so surprised he didn't say anything. Bella was beginning to worry when her mom flashed one of her best smiles.

"Nice to meet you, Trudy," she said warmly. "Bella has told us all about you. But are you sure you want to work on this old house on your day off?"

"Absolutely!" Trudy replied. "I spent a couple of years building houses in South America. I know my way around drywall and wet plaster. And there's nothing more rewarding than a little do-it-yourselfing."

Bella watched her mom's face carefully. She knew that look. It was the look she gave Bella when she wasn't sure if she should go along with something or not.

At that moment there was another knock on the door. Bella ran to open it and a man carrying an animal cage stepped inside.

"You must be Joe Saunders," Bella said.

"And you must be Bella," the man answered.

Bella liked him right away. His brown eyes had soft lines around them and he wore a red baseball cap.

"Can't say I'm surprised to see you here, Trudy," he said. He gave the librarian a hug. "I knew you wouldn't be able to stay away from this old house."

Joe looked over at Bella's parents. "She knows this house better than anyone in town. And she's a natural with a hammer, too."

Trudy smiled. "Here to take care of that skunk, Joe?" she asked. "She's probably Penelope Underhouse's great-great-granddaughter."

Joe laughed. "Penelope Underhouse was the skunk that lived in the basement when Trudy was a little girl," he explained.

"We called her P. U. for short," Trudy smiled shyly.

"The name fit!" Joe laughed. "She was a smelly one, all right. And stubborn. It wasn't easy to get rid of her."

"Why don't I take you downstairs?" Bella's mom suggested. "I can show you where P. U.'s heir seems to be living."

Bella's dad was looking closely at Trudy's tool belt. He looked kind of excited. "How about I take you up to the roof," he said to Trudy. "There are some sneaky leaks I'm having trouble finding."

Grinning from ear to ear, Bella followed her dad and her new friend Trudy outside. Her plan was working better than she'd imagined.

CHAPTER 8

Checking Out

Bella was not surprised when Trudy showed up the next day, too. Bella's mom and dad tried to turn her away. But Trudy insisted on staying.

"Bella and I are just getting started." Trudy bowed slightly and held out her hand to Bella. "Shall we?" she asked.

Bella grinned and linked her arm through Trudy's. Then the two of them skipped down the hall and out the door.

Joe showed up again too. "Howdy!" he called to Trudy. She sat on the roof in a giant sun hat, pounding nails.

"Still having trouble with the little stinker?" Trudy called down. Joe didn't answer. He was already in the basement.

"He couldn't find the skunk yesterday," Bella explained. "He set traps in the basement loaded with peanut butter and yogurt."

Half of Bella was hoping Little P. U. wasn't caught. She didn't like to see animals in cages. But she didn't like smelling them in her house, either.

Bella loaded a small bucket with shingles. She pulled on a rope and the bucket lifted up toward the edge of the roof. She and Trudy had rigged a pulley system so they wouldn't have to carry stuff up the ladder.

"Special delivery," Bella called as the bucket swung upward.

Suddenly Joe came running out of the basement storm door. He looked like he was crying. Bella wondered if it was because he still hadn't gotten P. U. A second later she knew it was because P. U. had gotten him!

Poor Joe slunk into his truck and started down the drive. "I'll be back," he called.

Bella felt terrible for Joe, but when she looked up at Trudy through the roof hole she couldn't help herself. They both started laughing. They kept laughing until Trudy had nailed the last shingle in place.

Two days later Joe still smelled bad. He was sitting in the Baxter kitchen holding a cage. His skin was red from too much scrubbing and he looked a little down.

"P. U.'s eaten almost all of the peanut butter." Bella handed him the nearly empty jar. "She

must like it," she said encouragingly.

"I know," Joe shook his head. "She loves it, but she just eats it and leaves. I don't know how she gets out of the cages!"

Upstairs Bella heard shuffling and bumping sounds. The thumps had been getting quieter lately. In just two days the roof was fixed, the front of the house was rewired, and the plaster patching was finished in several rooms.

Bella's mom had even stopped talking to the walls. Well, except the one she was currently plastering.

Trudy showed up right after lunch, just like she said she would. She'd been busy at the library. Instead of overalls, Trudy wore mechanic's coveralls with the sleeves built in. The name stitched over her pocket read DUKE.

"Duke-of-all-trades?" Bella's dad asked when she came into the kitchen.

Trudy just smiled. "Today I am an interior decorator," she said. "And I've come in search of my handy assistant."

Bella caught a glimpse of the book under Trudy's arm and leaped out of her chair. It was *Hang It All! A Non-wallflower's Guide to Wallpapering.* They were going to fix the mess she'd made in the room at the top of the stairs!

Bella looked at her dad to see if he noticed Trudy's book too. But he had his head deep inside the refrigerator. The top of a stalk of celery stuck out of his hand.

"What happened to all of the peanut butter?" he asked.

"I don't know why they call it hanging," Trudy mused.

Bella smoothed the last piece of wallpaper against the wall. She was careful not to leave any tiny bubbles under the surface. Putting up wallpaper was more like tricky sticking.

But it was much easier than last time. Trudy was a big help. The two stepped back from the wall to admire their work. It looked good. *Really* good.

The roses fit together like a perfect puzzle. Bella couldn't even tell where the edges of paper were!

"Well done!" Trudy said seriously. She offered her hand to Bella for a shake.

"Bravo!" Bella replied. She tried to grip Trudy's hand like a serious businessperson. And she tried to keep the smile off of her face.

Bella heard footsteps in the hall. "Bella, it's almost time for dinner," her mom said. "Do you know where . . ."

Nellie Baxter trailed off. She stood silently in the newly papered room. She could not take her eyes off the roses. "Wow!" she whispered. "You two have been busy!"

Barnaby came in next. "Has anyone noticed that this room is in full bloom?" he asked.

"Bella did it," Trudy said. She started to gather up her stuff.

Bella's mom and dad squished her into a big hug. "Bella, it's beautiful!" Nellie said.

"I know it's been crazy lately. We've been

working so hard. Just two days until we open, and you know what? I think we might be ready!"

Bella felt the smile on her face grow bigger. It felt good to have her regular mom back!

"You've been such a big help, tulip," Barnaby added. He ruffled Bella's hair.

"And you," Nellie said, looking at Trudy. "Why don't you stay for dinner?"

Trudy looked at Bella. Her eyes were asking, "Is it safe?"

"I'm getting pizza," Bella's dad said.

Bella gave Trudy a thumbs-up.

"I'd be glad to." Trudy put down her bag and brushed off her coveralls.

"Excuse me!" a voice called from outside. "Your first guest is ready to check out!"

Bella ran down the stairs to the screen door.

Joe Saunders stood in the driveway. He was holding one of his traps, and pacing back and forth inside it was Little P. U. herself.

"You probably shouldn't come out to say good-bye," Joe called up. "But P. U. here just wanted to let you know how much she's enjoyed her stay."

"Where are you taking her?" Bella was relieved to see that P. U. was okay. In fact she was pretty cute. It was too bad she was so smelly.

"I'm going to drop her off in the woods outside of town," Joe said. "Then I'm going to take a long bath in spaghetti sauce!"

"Thank goodness you caught her," Bella's mom said.

"How did you finally do it?" Trudy asked.

"We ran out of peanut butter, but I found an old pancake under this bush," Joe pointed toward the porch. "It seemed to do the trick!"

CHAPTER 9

Checking Inn

Bella rolled over for the ten millionth time. Sleeping was impossible. She was too excited.

Bella grinned into her pillow. She still couldn't believe everything was ready.

After all the fixing there had been a ton of cleaning. There had been stairs to vacuum and beds to make. But she and her parents had done it. Well, with Trudy and Joe's help. The B & B was ready just in time. In the morning the first guests would arrive.

Bella listened to the sound of the waves outside her window. She let the noise drown out the ideas racing around in her brain. Finally her eyes closed. The next thing she knew sunlight was streaming in the window. Sea Inn was officially open for business!

Bella dressed quickly. There were still a few things she wanted to do before the guests arrived. Like her mom said, it was all in the details.

"Good morning," Bella's mom sang. Bella went skipping by. Nellie was making omelettes in the kitchen. "Try a taste?"

Bella hesitated. Then she opened her mouth to the forkful of cheesy eggs Nellie held out. She chewed slowly. Not her mom's best. But not her worst, either. Maybe the cooking curse was finally lifting.

Bella hurried to the small front office and opened the book of reservations. Under today's date there were two names:

Miss V. Mapleton Boston, Massachusetts
Gunnar Erickson Rejkavik, Iceland

Bella slammed the book shut and looked at the clock. Not enough time for real research. She was going to have to wing it.

She'd gotten the idea yesterday. She was looking at a book on the dining room table, *The Inn-Sider.* It suggested that you give each guest the comforts of their own home. And that was just what Bella intended to do.

Boston. Bella marched back to the kitchen. She opened the big pantry and scanned the shelves until she spied what she wanted.

Perfect. There were three cans of Boston baked beans. Bella took one out and raced upstairs to the Rose Room. She put the can of beans next to the flowers on the dresser. That ought to make Miss Mapleton happy!

Now what could she do for Gunnar Erickson? While she ate her breakfast, Bella thought about Iceland. She didn't know much about it. But it sounded cold. Maybe Mr. Erickson needed to warm up. That was it! He needed a hot bath.

Bella gobbled her breakfast and dashed upstairs to the third floor. The room up there had a private bathroom with a tub. Perfect for a hot bath before lunch!

The pipes thumped a little as the tub filled. The steamy water looked inviting. Bella thought it would look even better with some bath salts. She was on her way to get them when she heard honking.

The first guest had arrived!

Outside, a small gray lady stepped out of a long black car. There was a mean-looking man standing next to her. Bella thought it might be her husband.

"Welcome!" Bella's mom wiped her floury hands on a towel. She offered one to the lady. The lady did not take it.

"I'm Barnaby Baxter," Bella's dad said. He was smiling his best smile. "This is my wife, Nellie. And you are our first guest!"

The lady sniffed. "I am Miss Mapleton," she said crisply. She did not sound very excited to be the first guest. And she did not introduce the man next to her. Maybe he wasn't her husband.

"I'm Bella," Bella said. She stepped right up to Miss Mapleton and smiled.

"I didn't know children were allowed to stay here," Miss Mapleton said. Her mouth was a thin line.

"Oh, I'm not staying," Bella explained. "I live here."

Miss Mapleton's line turned into a frown.

"I work here too." Bella went on. She tried to lift Miss Mapleton's suitcase. All she could do was drag it a couple of inches. It was really heavy. Maybe Miss Mapleton brought her own cans of beans.

"I'll get that." Bella's dad lifted the bag.

"*I'll* get that," the stern man said. He reached for the bag. "I carry madame's bags. If you would be so kind as to show me to her room?"

Bella's eyes got wide. The man wasn't her husband. He was her butler! Miss Mapleton had a real live butler!

Miss Mapleton went to the office with her parents. Bella took the butler up to the Rose room. It looked as good as she remembered. She spread her arms to show it off and did a little twirl.

"Lovely," the butler sniffed. He lifted the case onto the bed. It landed with a soft squelch. The bed was soaking wet! But how . . .

Bella and the butler looked up at the same time. Water was dripping from the ceiling.

"Oops!" Bella took the butler by the hand. "Wrong room! I forgot we're watering in there today."

Bella led the butler to a room across the hall. She threw open the door and pointed inside. She didn't wait to see how he liked it.

She raced upstairs to Mr. Erickson's bathroom. It was filled with steam . . . and water. Bath water was streaming over the edge of the tub. Bella sloshed over to turn off the tap. Then she sat on the edge of the tub. Water soaked into her seat. The whole room was flooded!

CHAPTER 10

Home Cooking

Bella pulled the towels off the rack and began to sop up the water. She felt a lump in her stomach. She really didn't want her mom and dad to find out what had happened. But there was no way she could keep this a secret! And she needed help. Bella walked slowly down to tell her parents.

Nellie was humming in the kitchen. Bella's lump got bigger. Things were finally going right. How could she tell her mother what she had done?

Bella turned and sprinted out the door.

It didn't take long to run the two blocks to the library. Inside, it was empty. Bella could hear Trudy shuffling through the books in the back.

Nibbling on her fingernail, Bella leaned on Trudy's desk and caught her breath. She wondered if there was a book for a girl whose life was turning into a disaster. Maybe something in the 158s.

Finally Trudy emerged. Bella had planned to explain what had happened and ask for advice. But as soon as she saw her friend her voice caught in her throat. Her eyes overflowed just like the tub in Gunnar's room.

Trudy did not hesitate. She hopped over her desk. Taking Bella by the hand, she led her outside. Then she used the pencil she kept behind her ear to write a quick note on a Post-it: EMERGENCY. BACK SOON. She stuck it on the door and locked it.

On the short walk back, Bella told Trudy everything.

"Do you think the plaster ceiling will be ruined?" she asked. Her mom had worked so hard!

"I think there's some plaster left," Trudy assured her. "We can fix that later. Let's just get things dried up, huh?" Trudy used the corner of her shirt to wipe a leftover tear off of Bella's cheek.

A big blue sedan was parked in Sea Inn's circular drive. It had to be Mr. Erickson's! Trudy saw the panicked look in Bella's eyes. They ran to the other side of Sea Inn and up the narrow back stairs.

Trudy flattened herself against a wall and made sure the coast was clear. Then she motioned Bella into the hallway.

"Towels!" Trudy hissed.

Bella stooped low and walked as quietly as she could. She was on a secret mission. She opened the linen closet and dug for the old towels in the back. She tossed a few to Trudy, who put one on as a disguise.

Bella's mom was greeting Mr. Erickson downstairs. "What brings you to Sandyport, Mr. Erickson?"

"Please, call me Gunnar," a man's voice replied. "I came for some sun."

"It must be cold in Iceland," Nellie Baxter said in her pleasant voice.

"Not as cold as Greenland," Gunnar joked.

Bella wanted to stay and listen. But she had a job to do. She dashed up the last flight of stairs.

Trudy let out a low whistle when she saw the wet room. "It's just water," she said, waving her hand.

The sopping up didn't take long. Trudy drained the tub. They hung the bath mat to dry. And Bella replaced the towels she used earlier. They were just closing the door when Bella's mom opened it for Mr. Erickson.

"Just finished up in here, ma'am," Trudy said. She had tied her towel disguise around her waist. She pushed Bella and her pile of wet towels ahead of her into the hallway.

"Ah, maid service," Gunnar smiled. "Very nice."

Cleanup in the Rose Room was trickier. The wet bedding had to be changed and the mattress taken out to dry. It was a big job. But Bella was used to those now. While Bella took the wet things to the laundry, Trudy checked the ceiling.

"Nothing a little paint won't fix when it's dry," she announced.

"What, more fixing?" Nellie poked her head in. "I thought Miss Mapleton was staying in here." Bella's mom looked confused. Then she looked at the water-stained ceiling. "What in the–"

"Mom, I, uh . . ." Bella didn't know where to start.

"She wet the bed," Trudy said in a very serious voice.

That's when Bella cracked up. She laughed so hard she almost *did* wet the bed. She laughed until her side hurt and she couldn't laugh anymore. Then she told her mom the whole story.

"You've been working so hard I didn't want you to be mad. I didn't mean to mess things up."

"Oh," Bella's mom pulled her into a hug. "You've been such a big help. How could I be mad at you? What I need to do is thank you. And you, too, Trudy. I think what we need is an opening day celebration!"

Bella saw a look in her mom's eyes that she hadn't seen in a while. A look Bella had missed.

Trudy and Bella followed Nellie down to the kitchen. Nellie was talking to herself again, but in a good way. "Flowers. Lots of flowers. Ice. We'll need ice. Lemons. And homemade ice cream? No, bread pudding. Rhubarb maybe."

"Mom, are you going to cook?" Bella asked cautiously. "For the guests?"

"Of course!" Bella's mom replied.

At seven dinner was served.

The dining room looked elegant. The chande-

lier had real candles burning in it, and in the dim light the food at least *looked* delicious.

Along with Trudy and Joe and Bruno the baker, the Baxters had invited the Sea Inn guests to join in their celebration dinner. Bella was surprised to see even grouchy Miss Mapleton had agreed. Her butler stood solemnly behind her chair until

Barnaby insisted he take a seat at the table.

"Everybody eats together at my house," Bella's dad said.

It was hard not to notice how nervous Bella's dad looked when Nellie brought out the main dish: lasagna. Trudy seemed skeptical too.

"Here is to a grand, grand opening," Trudy said. She raised her glass of sparkling apple cider in a toast.

Bella crossed her fingers under the table. If the meal was as bad as Bella feared, Sea Inn's first official day might also be its last!

"It is a beautiful inn," Gunnar raised his glass and nodded. "And so clean."

Trudy kicked Bella gently under the table.

The plates were passed. Bella took lots of salad and garlic bread. Just in case. Then she took a medium-size piece of lasagna.

Cautiously, she took a bite and chewed. It was good. No, delicious!

At the head of the table, Barnaby swallowed. A slow grin spread across his face.

"This tastes just like the lasagna my mother made." Miss Mapleton actually smiled. Everyone looked up, surprised. She held her fork in the air, closed her eyes, and sighed. "It tastes like home."

Bella couldn't agree more.

Don't miss Bella's next adventure in
Bella Baxter and the Itchy Disaster!

CHAPTER 1

Plant Plan

Shredded Nuggets plunked into Bella's cereal bowl. They sounded dusty. Bella added milk. They still tasted dry.

Oh well, Bella thought. *At least it will keep me going until I can get to Bruno's–and the library.*

At the sink Nellie Baxter was splashing and clinking her way through the morning dishes. And she was humming!

It had been ages since Bella heard her mom

hum. Ever since the Baxter's moved into Sea Inn Nellie had been stressed out. Even her usually fantastic cooking had taken a nosedive. Just thinking about some of her mom's food disasters made Bella's Shredded Nuggets taste better.

Bella hummed along between bites. It was good to have her regular mom back. She hummed. She smiled. She laughed. And most important, she cooked like she used to.

"Can you take the compost out when you're done?" Nellie asked.

Bella's grin faded. Her back-to-normal mom was constantly giving her chores. And if Bella's to-do list kept growing, she'd never make it to the library.

Bella popped the last shred of nugget into her mouth. The name Frederick Fauna spun around in her head. How was she going to welcome him? What would make a plant scientist feel at home?

Bella carried her bowl to the sink and grabbed the compost bucket. It was full of slimy eggshells, food scraps, and coffee grounds.

Bella's dad insisted that all those food scraps needed was a few months in a big stinky pile full of worms and other creepy crawlies. After that, the whole mess would make a super vitamin shake for his garden. And Barnaby Baxter was passionate about his garden.

Being careful not to spill, Bella carried the heavy bucket onto the front porch. She rounded the house and scampered down the steps to the backyard.

The front of Sea Inn had flowerbeds and two patches of lawn. The back was wild. The woods practically grew up to the porch. There were paths leading in several directions. One of them, the one Bella was on, led to an old shed circled in chicken wire. Just inside the wire was the compost pile.

"Here you go, worms," Bella said. She tipped the bucket upside down next to a patch of pretty purple flowers.

"I guess you wild flowers like this compost stuff too." Bella leaned down to get a closer look.

She had never seen the tiny flowers before. Being careful not to touch the rotting compost, she picked a few.

Suddenly Bella stood up straight. She dropped her bucket and looked around at all of the plants growing wild around her. "That's it!" she told the blossoms gleefully. "I can fill Dr. Fauna's room with local plants!"

With the bucket in one hand and the purple flowers in the other, Bella started back up the path. Her plan was perfect! Dr. Fauna would feel right at home surrounded by plants. After all, they were his life's work!

Bella hadn't gotten far when she noticed another pretty plant by a stand of birch trees. It had shiny rosy leaves that grew in groups of three. She picked a branch. She stopped again, by the porch, for a red and yellow flower with long pointy petals. And again for a tiny yellow flower with round petals nestled between two rocks.

Bella's mind raced. She pictured all kinds of plants in vases on Dr. Fauna's windowsill. She could even label them! ITTY-BITTY PURPLE PRETTIES. SHINY TINY LEAF TRIO. It would be fun to think up her own names. But since Dr. Fauna was a botanist he'd probably be more interested in the plants' real names.

Bella clutched her bouquet and ran the rest of the way to the house. She didn't know the real names of any of the plants she was holding. Lucky for Dr. Fauna, research was her specialty!